Dear Parent:

Congratulations! Your child is taking the first steps on an exciting journey. The destination? Independent reading!

STEP INTO READING® will help your child get there. The program offers five steps to reading success. Each step includes fun stories and colorful art. There are also Step into Reading Sticker Books, Step into Reading Math Readers, Step into Reading Write-In Readers, Step into Reading Phonics Readers, and Step into Reading Phonics First Steps! Boxed Sets—a complete literacy program with something for every child.

Learning to Read, Step by Step!

Ready to Read Preschool–Kindergarten
• big type and easy words • rhyme and rhythm • picture clues
For children who know the alphabet and are eager to begin reading.

Reading with Help Preschool–Grade 1
• basic vocabulary • short sentences • simple stories
For children who recognize familiar words and sound out new words with help.

Reading on Your Own Grades 1–3
• engaging characters • easy-to-follow plots • popular topics
For children who are ready to read on their own.

Reading Paragraphs Grades 2–3
• challenging vocabulary • short paragraphs • exciting stories
For newly independent readers who read simple sentences with confidence.

Ready for Chapters Grades 2–4
• chapters • longer paragraphs • full-color art
For children who want to take the plunge into chapter books but still like colorful pictures.

STEP INTO READING® is designed to give every child a successful reading experience. The grade levels are only guides. Children can progress through the steps at their own speed, developing confidence in their reading, no matter what their grade.

Remember, a lifetime love of reading starts with a single step!

For Andrew, Shelby, Anna, Max, and Lucy
—A.J.H.

To Elaine
—H.W.S.

Text copyright © 2010 by Anna Jane Hays
Illustrations copyright © 2010 by Hala Wittwer Swearingen

Visit us on the Web!
www.stepintoreading.com

Educators and librarians, for a variety of teaching tools, visit us at
www.randomhouse.com/teachers

Library of Congress Cataloging-in-Publication Data
Hays, Anna Jane.
Spring surprises / by Anna Jane Hays ; illustrated by Hala Wittwer Swearingen.
    p. cm. — (Step into reading. Step 2 book)
Summary: A rhyming tribute to the wonders brought by spring.
ISBN 978-0-375-85840-6 (trade pbk.) — ISBN 978-0-375-95840-3 (lib. bdg.)
[1. Stories in rhyme. 2. Spring—Fiction.] I. Swearingen, Hala Wittwer, ill. II. Title.
PZ8.3.H3337Sp 2010
[E]—dc22 2009013383

Printed in the United States of America

10 9 8 7 6 5 4 3 2

Spring Surprises

A STICKER BOOK

by Anna Jane Hays

illustrated by Hala Wittwer Swearingen

Random House 🏠 New York

Wake up, wake up!
Spring is here,
calling us outside.
Frosty winter,
say goodbye!

Hello, blue sky,
where birds fly high
and clouds puff by.

The groundhog has come up to stay.

The bear cub has come out to play.

Welcome, sunshine,
warm our cheeks.
Melt the snow and
fill the creeks.

Welcome, wind,
come fly our kites!

Greet longer days
and shorter nights.

Dance with raindrops
in spring showers.

Watch buds open
into flowers.

Come discover
spring's surprises.

Pick and smell
the pretty prizes.

Make mud pies
to bake on rocks.

Make dollies
out of hollyhocks.

In the pond,

count pollywogs.

Watch them all

turn into frogs.

See the duckling
learn to swim.
Mother duck
is proud of him.

Look up, look up!

What's in the nest?

Climb up and peek.

Hop like bunnies,

hide and seek.

Robins bathe
in a puddle.
Little mouse
has to scuttle!

Hello,
yellow baby chicks,
calf that licks,
kid that kicks.

Welcome,

woolly little lamb.

You all are part of

spring's grand plan.

The sun stays up
so we can play
until late in
this spring day.

When stars pop out
in the night sky,
spring sings a loving
lullaby.

Bullfrogs croak,
owls *WHO-WHO*.
That is all
this day can do.